A NOTE TO PARENTS

Learning to recognize feelings and finding appropriate ways to express them are important steps in any child's growth. Pretending can be a big help to children as they work to understand more about feelings, but grownups sometimes need to clarify for children just where pretend stops and reality begins. That's one reason why, in both our storybooks and television programs, we keep the Neighborhood of Make-Believe separate from our "real" neighborhood. In Make-Believe, we pretend about certain things that couldn't happen in real life…and make it clear that that's what we're doing.

Each book in this series tells a story about feelings. Some of those feelings are happy ones and some aren't—jealousy and anger, for instance. Strong feelings can be hard to talk about, but pretending about them can make it easier. We hope that these stories will help you talk about feelings in *your* family. Though the stories are only make-believe, the feelings are real, and children need to know that having feelings of all kinds is a very real part of what makes us human beings.

Fred Rogers

Random House  New York

Copyright © 1987 Family Communications, Inc. All rights reserved under International and Pan-American Copyright
Conventions. Published in the United States by Random House, Inc., New York, and simultaneously in Canada by Random
House of Canada Limited, Toronto. Mister Rogers' Neighborhood, the Neighborhood Puppets and Neighborhood Trolley and
Design are trademarks of Fred M. Rogers.

Library of Congress Cataloging-in-Publication Data:
Rogers, Fred. Wishes don't make things come true. On cover: Mister Rogers' neighborhood.
SUMMARY: A visit to the Neighborhood of Make-Believe shows us that wishes don't make things happen,
people make things happen.
[1. Wishes—Fiction.   I. Sustendal, Pat, ill.
II. Mister Rogers' neighborhood (Television program) III. Title.   PZ7.R63Wi 1987 [E] 87-4447 ISBN: 0-394-88780-8 (trade
0-394-98780-2 (lib. bdg.)

Manufactured in the United States of America 1 2 3 4 5 6 7 8 9 0

A STORY FROM

MISTER ROGERS' NEIGHBORHOOD®

Wishes Don't Make Things Come True

By Fred Rogers

Illustrated by Pat Sustendal

Did you ever think that wishing for something could make it happen? Well, wishes *don't* make things come true, even though sometimes it may seem like they do. When people get mad, they might make mad wishes—but even mad wishes can't make scary things happen!

We could pretend about wishes in the Neighborhood of Make-Believe.

Ready, Trolley? Good. Let's go to the Neighborhood of Make-Believe!

It was a windy day in the Neighborhood of Make-Believe. Grandpère carefully propped up a picture outside the Eiffel Tower, where he lived. It was a picture of his granddaughter Collette, who was coming for a visit—and Grandpère was excited.

X the Owl and Henrietta Pussycat
could see Collette's picture from their
home in a nearby tree.

"Oh, that sure is a pretty little tiger cat," said X.
"Don't you think so, Hen?"

Henrietta didn't answer. She liked to think that
she was the prettiest cat in the neighborhood.

Everywhere Henrietta went that day she heard people talking about Collette.

"Such a sweet-looking little tiger!"

"How lucky Grandpère is!"

"Did you see her picture? What fancy hair and clothes!"

Henrietta didn't like the picture at all.
"Meow wish they'd notice *me*," she thought.
"Meow wish I meow fancy like Collette!"

So Henrietta went home
and looked through her
closet. She found a frilly
dress, a lacy hat, a shiny
necklace, and some
makeup. "Meow'll show
everyone who's fancy!" she
said to herself. Just
then there was a knock
at her door.

It was X the Owl and Daniel Striped Tiger.
"Why, Hen, you sure are all fancied up!" said X.
"And you look very pretty to me," Daniel added.
Henrietta smiled. She had wished to be fancy
and her wish had come true!

"Come with us to meet Collette when she arrives on the trolley," X said to Henrietta.

Henrietta shook her head. "Meow'll meet you at the castle later."

But on Henrietta's way to the castle, the wind messed up her fur and blew her hat crooked. By the time she got there, Henrietta didn't feel fancy anymore at all.

Collette's picture was now at the castle, along with a sign that read WELCOME COLLETTE.

The more Henrietta looked at Collette's picture, the worse she felt.

"Meow picture...a welcome sign... everything's meow Collette," Henrietta said. "Meow not fair. Meow wish—meow wish that picture meow fall down. Meow now!"

As she spoke the picture shook back and forth on its stand. And then...

Crash! The picture tumbled over and fell to the ground.

"Oh, meow!" Henrietta gasped. She clasped her paws over her eyes. "It's all meow fault. Meow made the picture fall. Meow wish came true!"

Someone patted Henrietta on the shoulder. It was Cornflake S. Pecially.

"I heard what you said, Henrietta, but I don't think wishing for something can make it come true. It just seems that way sometimes."

"Corney's right, Toots!" said Lady Elaine Fairchilde, popping up on the castle porch. "It was the wind that made the picture fall. It wasn't your wishing. The wind has blown stuff down all over the Neighborhood."

"But meow picture fell just when meow wished it would!" Henrietta said. She could see Grandpère and Collette approaching in the distance. "Meow don't want to be here meow everyone gets mad," she added. "Meow going home right now!"

And off she ran.

"Welcome to our neighborhood," King Friday XIII said to Collette when she and Grandpère arrived at the castle.

"*Merci*," said Collette. "I am feeling *très* welcome already!"

"We are *all* glad you came, my dear granddaughter," said Grandpère. Then he looked around and asked, "Where is the big picture we had of Collette?"

"The wind blew it down," explained Lady Elaine, holding the broken frame. "But now that we can see Collette in person, who needs a picture?"

Collette smiled. "I am looking forward to meeting all of the neighbors, Your Majesty," she said, turning to the king. "May I give a party for the whole neighborhood?"

"A lovely idea," said the king. "You may invite everyone."

"Oh, good!" said Collette. "Come, mon grandpère, let us go home and make party hats for all the guests."

When Daniel stopped by the Eiffel Tower a little later to say hello, Collette told him about the party. "I have not met all of the neighbors yet," she explained, "so would you please deliver these party hats to everyone for me?"

"I would be glad to," Daniel said.

Daniel went to the Museum-Go-Round, to the Rockit Factory, to the castle, to X the Owl's tree. Everyone was excited to hear about the party.

But when Daniel shook
Henrietta's doorbell, she shouted,
"Meow away! Meow go away!"

But Daniel said, "I'm here to invite
you to Collette's party and to give
you a party hat."

Henrietta opened the door a crack.

"Meow not fair! Collette gets meow party, too!"
Henrietta said.

"It's not a party for Collette," said Daniel. "It's a party
Collette is giving for *us*."

But Henrietta said, "Meow don't care, meow not going.
And anyway, meow might make a wish and something scary
meow happen again."

"Not by wishing, you won't," Daniel said. "If you were really mad at King Friday, do you think you could make the castle fall down by wishing?"

Henrietta thought a minute. "Meow don't know...." she said.

"Or if I were really mad at you," Daniel continued, "do you think I could make your tree fall down by wishing?"

Henrietta thought another minute. Then she shook her head. "Meow think meow would have to cut it down. Or meow really big wind meow blow it down. But meow tree would *never* fall down meow wishing!"

Grandpère appeared just then.

"I need you, my little Henrietta," he said.

"No, meow don't," Henrietta said. "Meow have Collette."

"But that is why I need you," said Grandpère. "I wish you would be a special friend for Collette and introduce all the neighbors to her at the party. They all know you and like you."

"Meow *do* know everybody," Henrietta said slowly. "And meow would like to be meow special friend."

"Then you'll do it?" said Grandpère. "Oh, Henrietta, my thanks to you for making my wish come true!"

As Daniel and Henrietta skipped off after Grandpère, the trolley came by. "Meow going to meow special party, Trolley," Henrietta called. "Meow everybody meow coming."

And everybody was there.

Henrietta's wish to look fancy came true because she got all dressed up and made her wish come true. And she made Grandpère's wish come true, too, because she said she'd come to the party and help Collette, which is just what Grandpère wanted. So that's the way it is: *people* can make things happen, but *wishes* don't make things happen.

If you wonder about things like that, it's good to talk about them with the people you love. They're the ones who can best help you learn and help you grow.